Kylie Jean

Vacation Queen

by Marci Peschke

illustrated by Tuesday Mourning

PICTURE WINDOW BOOKS
a capstone imprint

Kylie Jean is published by Picture Window Books
A Capstone Imprint
1710 Roe Crest Drive
North Mankato, Minnesota 56003
www.mycapstone.com

Library of Congress Cataloging-in-Publication Data
Names: Peschke, M. (Marci), author. | Mourning, Tuesday, illustrator.
Peschke, M. (Marci) Kylie Jean.
Title: Vacation queen / by Marci Peschke ; illustrated by Tuesday Mourning.
Description: North Mankato, Minnesota : Picture Window Books, a Capstone imprint, [2017]
Series: Kylie Jean
Summary: Mr. Carter is getting a newspaper award in New York City,
so Kylie Jean and her family set out across country on a driving vacation.
Identifiers: LCCN 2015050700
ISBN 978-1-5158-0058-3 (library binding)
ISBN 978-1-5158-0059-0 (paper over board)
ISBN 978-1-5158-0060-6 (ebook pdf)
Subjects: LCSH: Vacations—Juvenile fiction. | Automobile travel—Juvenile fiction.
Families—Texas—Juvenile fiction. | Texas—Juvenile fiction. New York (N.Y.)—Juvenile fiction. | CYAC:
Vacations—Fiction. | Automobile travel—Fiction. | Family life—Texas—Fiction. | Texas—Fiction. | New York
(N.Y.)—Fiction. Classification: LCC PZ7.P441245 Vac 2017 | DDC 813.6—dc23 LC record available at
http://lccn.loc.gov/2015050700

Creative Director: *Nathan Gassman*

Graphic Designer: *Sarah Bennett*

Editor: *Shelly Lyons*

Production Specialist: *Kathy McColley*

Design Element Credit:
Shutterstock/blue67design

Printed and bound in China.
009514F16

For Jackson, with love!
I see many fun road trips in your future!
— MP

Table of Contents

All About Me, Kylie Jean!

My name is Kylie Jean Carter. I live in a big, sunny, yellow house on Peachtree Lane in Jacksonville, Texas, with Momma, Daddy, and my two brothers, T.J. and Ugly Brother.

T.J. is my older brother, and Ugly Brother is . . . well . . . he's really a dog. Don't you go telling him he is a dog. Okay? I mean it. He thinks he is a real true person.

He is a black-and-white bulldog. His front looks like his back, all smashed in. His face is all droopy like he's sad, but he's not.

His two front teeth stick out, and his tongue hangs down. (Now you know why his name is Ugly Brother.)

Everyone I love to the moon and back lives in Jacksonville. Nanny, Pa, Granny, Pappy, my aunts, my uncles, and my cousins all live here. I'm extra lucky, because I can see all of them any time I want to!

My momma says I'm pretty. She says I have eyes as blue as the summer sky and a smile as sweet as an angel. (Momma says pretty is as pretty does. That means being nice to the old folks, taking care of little animals, and respecting my momma and daddy.)

But I'm pretty on the outside and on the inside. My hair is long, brown, and curly.

I wear it in a ponytail sometimes, but my absolute most favorite is when Momma pulls it back in a princess style on special days.

I just gave you a little hint about my big dream. Ever since I was a bitty baby I have wanted to be an honest-to-goodness beauty queen. I even know the wave. It's side to side, nice and slow, with a dazzling smile. I practice all the time, because everybody knows beauty queens need to have a perfect wave.

I'm Kylie Jean, and I'm going to be a beauty queen. Just you wait and see!

Chapter One
Bored!

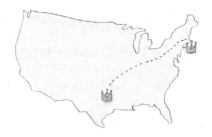

I wake up and stretch. Ugly Brother stretches out his doggie arms and legs, too. Looking out the window, I see the sun is already glowing like a fireball in the sky.

Yup, it's going to be another hot Texas summer day. Last summer we had one hundred days over one hundred degrees! This year we may hit that again. I bet it will be hot enough today to fry an egg on our sidewalk!

Before school got out, I thought that summer vacation would never come. It finally came, and now I'm bored. Last week I got to hang out with Ugly Brother and my best cousin, Lucy, every day, all day long. We went to the pool, canned tomatoes at Nanny and Pa's Lickskillet Farm, and even made jewelry with Granny. Now it's Monday, and I can't think of a single thing I want to do.

Sitting on the edge of my bed, I dangle my legs. "If I tell you a secret, will you promise not to tell anyone?" I ask my dog brother.

Ugly Brother barks loudly. "Ruff, ruff!"

Two barks mean yes. He loves a good secret.

I lean over to whisper in his ear, but he licks my face before I can say anything. Silly doggie! I pluck a tissue, dab off the drool, and try again.

"I wish I had school today," I whisper.

Ugly Brother whines and puts his paws over his eyes.

"I know, I know," I say. "Kids are supposed to love summer vacation, but I miss my friends, my teacher, and my bus driver, Mr. Jim."

Besides, there's nothing fun left to do. Sighing, I pick up my library book. I picked a book about a mouse for the public library's summer reading club. The mouse on the cover is floating along on a little boat, about to have an adventure.

Just then an idea hits my brain like a train zooming on a track. "Ugly Brother," I say. "I just figured out what's wrong! There are a lot of things to do right here in our little town, but I'm craving a *big* adventure!"

He barks, "Ruff, ruff."

Ugly Brother jumps off the bed and runs in a circle while chasing his tail. I think he would like to have an adventure, too. But it seems our summer is probably going to be filled with all of the same old things.

We watch TV all morning. Later that afternoon, Ugly Brother and I take my book to the backyard hammock. While we swing, I read out loud so Ugly Brother can hear the story, too. Pretty soon, he starts to snore. He is not being a good listener!

I start to daydream about different adventures we could go on. First I think about going to the Australian Outback and wrestling a crocodile. I lean over and wake up Ugly Brother.

"What would you think of a trip to the Outback?" I ask him.

Ugly Brother jumps off the hammock. He pretends he is a crocodile, chomping down with his big doggie teeth.

I laugh so hard that I fall out of the hammock. We roll around and wrestle until he ends up sitting on top of me.

"Maybe I'm not big enough to wrestle real crocs yet," I admit.

Next I imagine a space adventure. "We could go to space camp and sneak aboard a space shuttle," I suggest.

Ugly Brother cocks his head. He doesn't understand space camp.

I see Miss Clarabelle working in her flower bed, so I head over to tell her all about it.

"Hi, Miss Clarabelle," I say.

"Well, hello, Ms. Kylie," Miss Clarabelle answers.

"I have decided I want to go to space camp!"
I tell her.

Miss Clarabelle pulls weeds and listens.

"It will be amazing!" I exclaim. "I can wear
a space suit and float around the ship in zero
gravity, just like the characters did in a movie
I saw with T.J."

Miss Clarabelle says, "I'm sure you can do anything you set your mind to."

Just then I see Daddy pull in the driveway. He slowly parks the car. As he's opening the car door, he waves me over to help him out.

"Miss Clarabelle, we'll have to talk more about my big adventure later," I say. "Right now, Daddy needs my help."

"Come back tomorrow, and we'll talk more," she answers.

Chapter Two
Newspaperman News

I can see that Daddy is holding two familiar red-and-white bags. It must be a special occasion! He has Chinese takeout from China Express. The China Express restaurant is right downtown in an old gas station building. They painted it bright red like a fire engine, but it still looks like a gas station. Daddy likes it because it's right by the newspaper's office. Momma likes it because they have the best egg rolls in town.

Ugly Brother and I wave good-bye to Miss Clarabelle. Then we dash across the yard. Ugly Brother runs right to the front door, but I stop to help Daddy.

"Hi, Daddy," I say, smiling widely.

"Hello, sugar," says Daddy.

"Can I help carry a bag?" I ask.

"Thank you!" he replies. "That's a mighty nice offer." He hands me a bag. Then he puts his free arm around my shoulders. "I've got *big* news!" he adds.

"What is it?" I ask.

He winks and says, "Sorry, sugar, you'll have to wait until dinner. I want to tell everyone my news at the same time."

I am busy looking in the bag to see what we're having for dinner. When I see the famous egg rolls in their waxy wrapper, I smile widely. I decide I can wait until later for Daddy's big announcement.

Once we're in the kitchen, we put the bags on the counter. Daddy gives Momma a kiss hello while I start setting out the food. We have cashew chicken, beef with broccoli, fried rice, and (of course) egg rolls. We're going to eat family style. That means we all get a plate and put a little bit of everything on it. But T.J. always puts *a lot* of everything on his plate.

"T.J., dinner's ready," shouts Momma. "Wash up and come eat!"

"Yes, ma'am," he answers. "Be right there!"

I decide to fill my plate before he loads his up. Momma is right behind me. Daddy always waits until last.

When we are all sitting at the table, Daddy clears his throat. "I have exciting news," he says. "I am winning a B.N.A. — Better Newspaper Award! The best part is that the awards ceremony will be held in a very famous place: New York City!"

Momma jumps up and hugs Daddy.

T.J. shouts, "Way to go, Dad!"

I am happy for Daddy, too! My eyes are twinkling like jewels in a crown, because ever since I was itty bitty, I have wanted to see "The Queen of Liberty." After all, she has the biggest crown in all the land. I just *love* crowns!

"When do we leave?" I ask excitedly.

"I was planning on going by myself, but maybe we could make this a family trip," Daddy says.

"Yay!" I shout.

"Cool!" says T.J.

Momma says, "This is so exciting!"

Then we all talk about the trip while we finish eating our dinner. Daddy thinks that if the whole family goes, we should make it a road trip. After all, buying plane tickets for everyone would be very expensive!

T.J. has seconds and then asks, "Who's ready for a fortune cookie?"

"Me!" I reply.

I tear apart the plastic cookie wrapper and crack the golden cookie. A little white strip of paper flutters toward the floor.

"Oh, no!" I shout.

Ugly Brother is waiting to see if anything yummy will fall from the table into his mouth. Luckily, T.J.'s long arm comes to the rescue. He catches the paper just in time and hands it to me.

I read the fortune from the paper aloud. "You will journey to an exotic place."

"Oh, someday I'd like to go to Hawaii," says Momma.

"That sounds exotic," says Daddy.

I don't want to go to Hawaii, but I do want to take a trip. A journey means a trip! Even my fortune cookie knows I may be going on an adventure. I'm so excited that I don't even mind clearing the dinner table.

Chapter Three
Family Vacation

In the morning, I make a celebration breakfast for Daddy. I am proud of him for winning a big, important award. I put breakfast on a tray, along with a map of the United States that I drew and colored for a place mat. I drew a big pink crown right in the middle of New York City.

Ugly Brother helps me by staying out of the way while I carry the breakfast upstairs. I knock on the door. *Tip-tap.*

"Come in," Daddy says.

I walk in and set the tray next to Daddy. "Congratulations, Daddy!" I say.

"Thanks, sugar!" says Daddy. He starts digging in to the cereal, toast, and juice.

Momma looks at the tray. "That breakfast is only missing one thing," she says. "Coffee. I'm going to go make some, and I'll be right back."

"This is delicious!" Daddy says. "What's this map for?"

"I thought my map might help us plan our vacation," I answer. "Can I help plan our trip to see the Queen of Liberty?"

Daddy can't answer because his mouth is full.

"I'm glad you like your special breakfast, Daddy," I say.

When Momma comes back with the coffee, Daddy smiles. He says, "Kylie Jean would like to help plan our trip to New York City, and she'd like to see the Statue of Liberty."

"That sounds like a great plan," says Momma.

"I'll have to ask for some extra time off work," Daddy says.

"Today is Tuesday, and it will take some time to get there if we drive," says Momma. "I think we would need to leave on Thursday. That's not much time! Kylie Jean, we can use all the help we can get planning our trip!"

Daddy looks at Ugly Brother. "Sorry boy, but you're going to have to stay at the farm while we're gone," he says.

At first Ugly Brother is sad, but then Daddy gives him a bite of his toast.

I'm sad, too, until Daddy says, "I'm thinking we should bring Lucy along to keep Kylie Jean company on our trip."

"Hooray!" I shout.

Daddy says, "We'll have to ask her parents if it's okay."

I just know they'll say yes. The Carter family is going on vacation, and my best cousin, Lucy, is coming, too! Queen of Liberty, here we come!

* * *

Later that morning Momma takes our van to the garage for an oil change. I know she is doing it to get ready for our trip.

I stay home with T.J. I'm so excited to share my big news!

"T.J., can I pretty please run over to tell Miss Clarabelle my news about our trip?"

"All right, Lil' Bit," he says.

Miss Clarabelle is on her front porch. I run right up to her and blurt out, "Miss Clarabelle, I won't have time for space camp. I'm going on a family trip to New York City! I'm going to see the Queen of Liberty."

"Imagine that!" Miss Clarabelle says. "The Statue of Liberty is a wonderful site to see. I guess if you just wait, sometimes the adventure finds you! Please send me a postcard from the road."

I give her a big squeezy hug and promise to write from the road.

As soon as I get back home, the phone rings. I run over to pick it up. It's Lucy!

"I'm joining you on your trip to New York City!" she blurts out.

"Yay," I shout.

"I can't believe we are going on a road trip," she says.

"I can't believe I'm going to see the Queen of Liberty!" I reply.

"I know! It's so exciting!" she says.

"I'm going to help plan the trip, too!" I tell her.

"Maybe we can plan the route together," she suggests.

"Perfect!" I answer. "I'll call you later."

We both say, "Bye."

Just as I set down the phone, Momma walks in the door. I rush over to meet her. Before she can even set down her purse I ask, "Is it okay if Lucy helps me plan our trip?"

"Sure," she says, "but can you help me right now? I want to make a to-do list so we will be ready to leave on Thursday."

"Yup!" I agree.

I walk over to the kitchen, open a drawer, and grab a pen and paper. Momma starts unloading the dishwasher and naming off items for the list.

1. Pack suitcases.

2. Fill up the gas tank.

3. Make cookies and shop for snacks to put in a cooler.

4. Have T.J. get the camping gear ready.

5. Map a route.

6. Get cash from the bank.

7. Ask Miss Clarabelle to watch the house while we're away.

8. Ask Nanny and Pa to watch Ugly Brother.

It doesn't take long to make the entire list. Then I help Momma wash clothes so we will be ready to pack tomorrow. Finally, Momma and I make dinner. I just wish tomorrow would hurry up and get here!

Chapter Four
Pack and Plan

The next day when I wake up, the first thing
I see is an open suitcase on my bedroom floor.
Today is Wednesday. Tomorrow we will load our
van and head out for the Big Apple (that's a
nickname for New York City)! Leaning back on
my pillows, I think that I am one lucky girl who is
about to see the Queen of Liberty.

Ugly Brother stretches and then tumbles off the bed toward the suitcase. He stands there wagging his tail and looking at me.

I notice his doggie bone sticking out of the luggage. "Did you do some packing, too?" I ask.

He barks, "Ruff, ruff."

"You need your own bag, because you are going to Nanny and Pa's," I say.

I have a surprise for him! I jump out of bed and dig through my closet. Finally, I see my old pink duffel bag under some stuffed animals. I pull it out. It's the perfect bag for my doggie brother to pack his dishes and treats.

"Here is your very own suitcase!" I announce.

He runs over and licks me. That's his way of saying thank you.

We head downstairs to eat breakfast. Momma made pancakes and eggs. Just as we're finishing, Lucy knocks on the door.

"Come on in!" says Momma.

"Hi, Lucy," I say excitedly.

"Hi," she replies. "I thought I would stop over so we can plan the trip."

"Perfect!" I say. "Let's go upstairs."

We run up to my room and sit on the floor. Ugly Brother follows us.

"How many states do you think we'll go through on our trip?" I ask.

"Hmmm . . . maybe ten?" Lucy replies.

"I think it will be seven," I say.

Ugly Brother barks three times. He must think we will go through three states.

"Daddy has a United States road atlas. We can use it to count all the states on our route," I suggest.

"Good idea!" says Lucy.

I run and ask Momma to help us with the atlas. She finds it and opens it up to a map of the United States.

"First, we should find Jacksonville, Texas," Momma says. "Then we'll find New York City."

Looking over Momma's shoulder, Lucy and I count the states in between the two cities. We were both wrong! There are six states between Texas and New York.

"We will drive through six states, if we don't count Texas," I say. "Seven if we do, and that would make me right!"

We name the states as we point to the map.
"Arkansas, Tennessee, Virginia, Maryland,
Pennsylvania, and New York."

"This book has a map for every single state,
too," says Lucy.

"We better take this handy atlas on our trip,"
I add.

Then we decide to look at our travel route on
the Internet to see what fun stuff we can stop
and do on the way. Momma says the stops are
called tourist attractions. When I find the Crater
of Diamonds Park in Arkansas, I know we have to
stay there. I love bling, but Momma really loves it!

Then an idea hits my brain like a bright,
shiny sparkle on a gem. I think we should find a
special destination for everyone! So we do. From
diamonds to miniature golf, this trip is going to be
super exciting for the whole family.

The rest of the afternoon, Momma, Lucy, and
I bake cookies for the trip. Lucy and I mix in the
chocolate chips.

"I can't wait to see the Queen of Liberty!"
I say.

"Her real name is the Statue of Liberty,"
Momma says. "Have you packed enough clothes
and a special outfit for your visit to see her?"

"Yes, ma'am," I reply. "I have packed jeans,
shorts, T-shirts, sundresses, and a swimsuit. You
know my special pink, sparkly crown shirt? It's
going to be perfect for visiting the Queen."

"Yes, that shirt is just right!" says Momma.

Lucy chimes in, "When I get home, I want to
find something nice to wear, too."

Momma nods and takes a pan of hot chocolate
chip cookies out of the oven. The teapot clock on
the kitchen wall says four o'clock. Aunt Susie will
be here soon to pick up Lucy.

"Momma, can we please have a cookie before Lucy has to leave?" I beg.

"I suppose," Momma says, winking at us.

"Thanks," says Lucy as she chooses a warm cookie and takes a big bite.

"The next time I see you, we'll be picking you up for our vacation," I say to Lucy.

"I bet we don't sleep a wink tonight," she says, "not even if we count one hundred sheep!"

Just then, we hear Lucy's momma at the back door. While the mommas talk about last-minute details, we give Ugly Brother a treat. Then Aunt Susie says it's time to go.

"See you tomorrow, Lucy!" I shout. "In less than twenty-four hours we'll be hitting the road!"

* * *

In the early hours of the morning, when nighttime and daytime are still best friends, Momma wakes us up. It is the first day of our family vacation!

Chapter Five
Arkansas

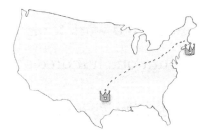

After a quick breakfast of cereal, we put our last-minute items into the van. Daddy loads the suitcases. We have almost everything!

Daddy is going to use his GPS, but I bring the handy United States road atlas, too. Lucy and I have come up with special destinations for each person in the family. I have shared all of the locations with Daddy, and he knows Momma's surprise destination is first!

We all pile into the van, and then we hit the road. In just seven days, I will finally get to see the Queen of Liberty!

Momma keeps reminding me that she's called the Statue of Liberty. I don't get it. Everyone can plainly see she's wearing a gigantic crown on her head! Queens wear crowns, so I prefer to call her the Queen of Liberty. I really wish I had a crown just like hers.

After a quick stop to pick up Lucy, we turn onto the highway. Lucy and I sit in the last row of seats in the van. T.J. is stretched out in the middle. Daddy and Momma are in the front. At first, we look out the windows. All we see are trees and more trees. We do live in the piney woods of east Texas, after all.

"I'm bored," says Lucy.

"Let's look in my bag for something fun to do,"
I answer.

We decide to color tiny fuzzy posters with
scented markers. T.J. is snoring from the middle
seat.

When we cross the state line from Texas to Arkansas, Daddy shouts, "Yee-haw!"

Lucy and I laugh. We want to join in, so we shout, too! "Yee-haw!"

Soon we stop in a town called Hope and have a sandwich for lunch.

I whisper in Daddy's ear, "How long will it take to get to Crater of Diamonds State Park from here?"

"From here, it's only about an hour's drive to Murfreesboro," Daddy whispers back. "Murfreesboro is right by the park."

After lunch, we drive and drive. It seems to take forever to get there! Finally, Daddy tells me we are in Murfreesboro. Soon we pull right up to the park.

I shout, "Momma, this is your special tourist attraction!"

"Who would like to go diamond hunting?" asks Daddy.

"I do!" Momma shouts.

"We do, too!" shout Lucy and I.

"Do I have to?" asks T.J. "I could just stay in the van."

"I would think that you'd want to be with your family," says Momma. "After all, this is a family vacation. Think of it as an adventure!"

Daddy rents five box screens at the park gift shop. They look like pie plates with screen doors on the bottoms. We will use them to sort the dirt away from the diamonds.

I buy a fun postcard to send to Granny and Pappy. Then the gift shop attendant gives us a park map, and we go hunting. At first no one finds anything. We dig and sift, dig and sift.

Then suddenly Momma screams, "I found a diamond! It's as tiny as a poppy seed, but it's really a diamond!"

She is jumping for joy. We are all excited.

"Fantastic!" Daddy says as he looks at the diamond.

We hunt for a long time, but Momma is the only one with any luck. By then, our whole crew is tired and sunburned. Daddy has reserved a park cabin, so we pack up and head that way.

When we get to our cabin, it is small but nice. It has a tiny kitchen, a couch, a picnic table, and three sets of bunk beds in it. Momma laughs and tells Daddy he has to sleep on the top bunk!

T.J. says, "I can sleep on the bottom or top of my bunk."

"Lucy, do you want to sleep on the top or the bottom?" I ask.

"I'll take the bottom," answers Lucy.

"Okay," I say.

Momma says, "Now that we've settled where everyone is sleeping, let's get dinner. You girls can help me!"

We unpack the cooler and make Frito pies in bags for dinner. Lucy helps Momma stir the chili. Once we fill the bags, I put the cheese on top. Then we all sit at the picnic table and eat. So far, it has been a great trip!

When we have finished eating and cleaning up, Momma tucks Lucy and me into our bunks.

"Thanks for a wonderful day!" she says. "Good night, little bugs."

"Good night," we say.

Then we giggle until Lucy falls asleep. I grab a flashlight and dive back under the covers. It's time to write Granny and Pappy's postcard. It's a card with a giant diamond on the front.

Dear Granny and Pappy,

We hunted for diamonds today! It was super fun. Guess who found a diamond? Momma did! I picked this card for you, Granny, because you love bling, just like Momma and me. We stayed in a real true cabin tonight, and I am sleeping in a bunk bed with Lucy. Tomorrow we are going to Tennessee. In just six days, I will see the Queen!

Love and kisses,
Kylie Jean

Chapter Six
Tennessee

In the morning, we load up and head out. When we reach the next town, we stop at the Waffle House to eat breakfast. Lucy and I share a berries and cream waffle. It's delicious!

Our big stop today will be Nashville, Tennessee. It will take us a long time to get there. As we're driving, I grab the road atlas to check our progress. We're traveling on Interstate 40. We still have a long way to go before we reach New York City!

Right before we get to Memphis, we come to a big bridge. It crosses the mighty Mississippi River.

"This is the biggest bridge I have ever been on!" I say.

"It has to be big enough to cross this river," says Momma.

"Who can spell *Mississippi* five times fast?" asks T.J.

Lucy and I are about to start spelling, but before we can try it, Daddy shouts, "Yee-haw!" as we cross the bridge.

"We're in a new state," says Momma. "This is Tennessee."

"Are we going to yell 'Yee-haw!' for every new state we visit?" I ask.

"I reckon so!" replies Daddy. "It's like saying *hello* to a new place."

On the other side of the bridge, we stop and take a picture of the river. The Mississippi is so wide, it almost looks like a lake.

Once we're on the road again, Lucy and I take turns asking how much longer it will take to get there. Momma finally gets sick of answering, so she starts a game of "I Spy." We play that, and then we color until we arrive in Nashville.

Our first stop in Nashville is our hotel. After we get settled, the whole family heads downtown to eat dinner at the Back Alley Diner. Momma drives this time, since this will be Daddy's special tourist destination.

The diner has a big neon sign. Inside, there is a wooden stage, and there is a band performing on it. The band members have guitars, banjos, a piano, and drums. They are a little loud.

"Daddy, this stop is for you!" I shout.

Daddy laughs, "You know how I love country crooners," he says.

Momma adds, "This place is supposed to have the best burgers in town, too."

"Finally, we get to do something really fun. I like this place!" T.J. says with a big smile.

Daddy and T.J. both order the double-stack bacon cheeseburger. When the waitress brings out their food, our eyes all pop. The hamburgers are almost as big as the plates! Daddy and T.J. look so excited to dig in.

The music has us all singing along. Daddy sings super loud. Grinning, Momma covers her ears. She likes to tease Daddy.

Then an idea hits my brain like a pick on a banjo string. "Can somebody please help me pick out a postcard before we leave?" I ask.

"I will, Lil' Bit," replies T.J. "I know just the one. It caught my eye when we came in."

T.J. and I make a stop at the front desk. He shows me a postcard with a giant guitar on the front. It's perfect! We quickly make our purchase.

Back at the hotel, I write a note to Nanny and Pa on the postcard. Then Lucy and I pile into a big bed together. T.J. sleeps on the couch. Momma and Daddy have the other bed. In no time at all, we're all fast asleep.

* * *

The next day is Saturday. It's a good day for a special pink outfit, because we're off to see a pink elephant! We head back out on Interstate 40 bright and early.

"I'm sure y'all are going to notice that I get two stops," I say. "It's only fair, because I planned the trip. It was a lot of work, even though Lucy helped. Pretty please keep your eyes open for a big sign for the Pink Elephant roadside attraction."

"It's right there!" Lucy shouts. "We need to take the next exit."

I spy a giant pink elephant trunk sticking up, so I shout, "I see the elephant!"

Lucy and I are so excited! We can hardly wait for the van to stop. When we pull into the parking lot beside it, I realize that the elephant is as big as a house. It's painted the color of bubble gum. Since the elephant is so tall and I'm so short, when I try to take a selfie I only get my face and the elephant's knees.

"Please, T.J., take my picture!" I beg.

"I want to be in the picture!" Lucy adds.

T.J. snaps our picture, and then we take a look at it. I'm glad I have on pink today, because I look mighty nice standing by that big pink elephant!

Back in the van, we realize that to get to Virginia today will be a lot of driving for Daddy. Momma decides we will spend the night at the local campground. After a short drive we reach our campground destination, Camper's Corner.

I ask, "Why is it called Camper's Corner when it isn't on a corner?"

Momma says, "Someone probably just thought it sounded nice."

Daddy and T.J. start to unload everything so they can set up the tent. Lucy and I help Momma organize our sleeping bags and pillows. Before long, everything is ready for us to get some shut eye, but first we start a campfire and roast some hot dogs for dinner. They're good with salty chips and cold soda from the ice chest.

Momma says, "This is my kind of meal. No clean up!"

Daddy adds, "I just like cooking over a fire."

T.J. and Lucy are still eating. I look at the dusky sky and remember I have a postcard to write! *Chomp!* I finish my hot dog in one big bite. It's a little hard to chew and swallow.

I say, "Momma, I'm done! Can I write a postcard to Nanny and Pa now?"

Momma says, "Okay, but keep it short. We have an early day tomorrow!"

I grab my pen from of my bag. The I settle in at the picnic table. I have lot to say, but a postcard is teeny tiny, so I have to think about what I want to say before I start to write it . . .

Dear Nanny and Pa,

Last night we stopped in Nashville at the Back Alley Diner to listen to country music singers. Lucy and I planned that stop for Daddy, but T.J. liked it, too. We all liked it! I hope Ugly Brother is doing fine. Please give him a kiss and tell him I miss him! Also, we went to see a big pink elephant. You know how I love pink! We are camping tonight, so I will be sleeping in a tent.

Love,
Kylie Jean
XOXO

P.S. I am texting you a picture of Lucy and me with the famous pink elephant.

Chapter Seven
Virginia

The next morning, we go to a church service in the campground before we head out to our next state. Momma thinks it's really nice for them to offer church on Sundays. After the service we pack up and go.

"How far to Virginia?" asks Lucy.

Daddy says, "Not too far, but then it will take us a while to get to the town of Herndon."

He's right! After we drive through Knoxville, we see the state line and a big sign that says Welcome to Virginia.

"Yee-haw!" we all shout.

We keep driving and driving. I keep checking my Virginia map to make sure we aren't getting lost. It seems to be taking a very long time to get to our destination. We stop at a few rest areas to stretch and walk around.

Back on the road, Lucy and I play cards. We like Go Fish and War. T.J. even likes to play War.

Finally, we roll into Herndon. We stop at a restaurant to eat a bucket of fried chicken for dinner. After we eat, Daddy drives us to a new campground.

T.J. helps Daddy put up the tent. "It seems like I just did this!" he complains.

Daddy nods. "Yes, it does, because we camped yesterday," he says. "The good news is we'll stay here tomorrow night, too."

Lucy and I help Momma unload the rest of the van. Then she gets busy organizing sleeping bags and pillows. The stars are starting to peek out around the edges of a dusky gray sky brushed with watermelon pink. Lucy and I sit at the picnic table talking about New York City.

"What do you think it will be like?" I ask.

"I don't know," Lucy replies. "I've never been to any city bigger than Dallas."

"Me either," I say. "It's going to be so exciting!"

T.J. interrupts us. "What's exciting is that tomorrow morning I'll get to play miniature golf."

"You're in for a treat," Momma says. "Kylie Jean picked a great course for you to play."

Daddy says, "I can't believe this is the last leg of our trip already."

"Okay, bedtime, everyone!" Momma says.

We all squeeze into our tent and try to get comfortable in our sleeping bags. It's a warm night, and there's a skeeter buzzing near my ear. Before long, Daddy and T.J. are having a snoring contest. I think Daddy wins!

After a quick breakfast the next morning, we go to The Jungle miniature golf course.

T.J. is sporty. He can play any sport you can name, but putt-putt golf is his favorite.

"This course looks just like the set of an Indiana Jones movie!" he says.

"Yup!" I say with a grin.

He is ready to get started, so he grabs his putter and jogs over to the first hole. The rest of us are slower. By the time we get there, T.J. is ready to go on to the next hole.

"I just made a hole in one!" he brags.

"Way to go, son!" Daddy says.

T.J. tells us to take our time. Of course, he avoids the crocodile and scores a perfect game!

Lucy and I jump when we see the crocodile. It looks real!

Next we see fake skeletons. "Look out, Lucy!" I shout.

"They're scary!" she shouts.

"Yes, but not as scary as those statues with glowing red eyes!" I say.

We try to ignore the snakes and wild boars. Then we see some apes.

"They look real, too. It sure is an adventure playing golf here!" says Lucy.

"I sure hope T.J. is having fun," I say. I look over to see him starting a new game. He's way ahead of us!

This place reminds me of the Outback adventure that Ugly Brother and I had thought about in the hammock. I tell Lucy all about it.

Laughing, she says, "I think we got that adventure after all!"

That night before bed, Lucy and I write a postcard to our friend Cara.

Dear Cara,

We are having a super FUN vacation! Today we went to play putt-putt golf with crocodiles. They weren't real, but they were still scary. Only three more days until we see the Queen of Liberty. We'll tell you all about our trip when we get back.

Your friends,
Kylie Jean and Lucy

Chapter Eight

Maryland

The next morning we leave bright and early for Maryland. Only two more days until I see the Queen! Today is Tuesday, and we don't have a special destination.

Lucy and I decide to play the license plate game to pass the time. We see a lot of Virginia plates, some from Tennessee and North Carolina, and one truck that passes us has Texas plates.

"They're from Texas!" I shout.

"Honk, honk!" adds Lucy.

Daddy honks, and we wave. They wave back!

It is hard to see all fifty states on one trip. It's not surprising that we never see plates for Hawaii. It's in the middle of the ocean! But we have seen plates for 32 of the fifty states. I've been keeping track on my notepad.

"Who can guess how many of the states' plates we have seen?" I ask.

But before anyone can answer, Daddy shouts, "Yee-haw!"

We are in Maryland! We stop at a rest area just across the state line.

"This is a very fancy rest area," Momma says.

"The building looks like the White House!"
I add.

"I guess they are trying to make a good
impression," says Daddy.

Soon we're back in the van and on the road
again. Just before we get to Hagerstown, we spot
a *giant* rocking chair, so we stop to take a look. It's
on top of a store. I can hardly believe it. The chair
is sixteen feet tall — almost as tall as our two-story
house!

"Can we stop?" I shout.

"Why not?" Daddy answers. "I could really use a break."

We all get out and walk around. Inside the store, they are selling postcards, souvenirs, and furniture. They have lots and lots of rocking chairs. The chairs come in all colors and sizes.

I decide to buy a postcard to send to Miss Clarabelle, and then we load back into the van.

"This has been an in-and-out stop!" says Daddy.

"The mother who sits in that rocking chair must have a giant baby!" jokes Momma.

Daddy laughs. "Would anyone like to go swimming?" he asks.

"We would!" Lucy and I shout.

"I don't know about swimming, but I'm ready to be out of this car!" Momma says.

Soon Daddy pulls into a hotel parking lot. We can see the big blue pool full of sparkly cool water.

We all help Daddy unload so we can get to the pool faster. Quick as a flash, we change clothes. T.J. is the first one out the door, but Lucy and I are right behind him.

At the pool, Lucy and I pretend to be mermaids while T.J. does cannonballs. The water splashes and gets our towels wet, but we're having so much fun, we don't care. After we finish swimming, it's time to get ready for bed. But first, I write Miss Clarabelle a note.

Dear Miss Clarabelle,

I remembered my promise to send you a postcard. We have had a lot of adventures on this trip. Today we saw a giant rocking chair just like the ones on your front porch. Now imagine them as big as a house. That's how big this rocking chair was!

I am going to see the Queen of Liberty in one more day. I will bring you a souvenir from New York City. I miss you and your sweet puppy, Tess. I miss Ugly Brother, too.

Hugs,
Kylie Jean

Chapter Nine

Pennsylvania

It's Wednesday, and we are headed for Lucy's stop at the Crayola Experience in Easton, Pennsylvania. Pretty soon we see a large blue sign that says Pennsylvania: The Keystone State.

We all shout, "Yee-haw!"

"Why is it called The Keystone State?" I ask.

Daddy explains, "Because it was an important original colony — one of the first thirteen."

Lucy is not thinking about keystones. "I can't believe I'm about to see the world's largest crayon!" she says.

"I wonder if it's going to be as big as the rocking chair we saw," I add.

"No way!" says T.J. "That chair was huge."

"Just wait and see," Momma says.

Lucy and I try to read our books, but it's hard to concentrate. Finally, we arrive at the Crayola Experience. Everything is colorful, even the parking lot signs. Once we get inside, we buy our tickets.

"It looks like a rainbow exploded in this building," T.J. says.

Looking around, I decide T.J. is right. It's extremely colorful in here! First we watch a little movie about how they make the crayons. They have giant pots of hot wax. Then they pour powder and pigment into the wax.

"What is pigment?" I ask.

"That's what makes the color," Momma replies. "It's like the dye we use for Easter eggs."

"Oh," I say, "then I wish they would always use pink pigment!"

"I would like it if they only made lavender crayons," Lucy says. "I like purple best."

We watch while the wax goes into a bucket. They pour it into trays filled with little round holes. The trays are called molds. The molds form the wax into crayon shapes. When the crayons are pushed back up, they pop out of the molds.

"It's like magic!" Lucy says. "One minute they are runny wax, and the next they are crayons."

Daddy likes the part of the movie with the labeling machine. I think the machine reminds him of his newspaper company's printing press. After the crayons get a label, they go in a box with other crayons to keep them company.

When the movie is over, Momma asks, "What was your favorite part, girls?"

"I liked seeing the crayons pop up out of the mold," I say.

"My favorite part was when they put the coloring in the wax," says Lucy.

On the way out of the room, we each get our very own box of crayons! Then we go into a room that is like a crayon museum. It has all of the old crayon colors.

"Oh, look!" Momma says. "These are some of the colors Daddy and I colored with when we were little!"

T.J. pretends to be bored, but I can tell he likes looking at the crayons.

In the Crayola Craft room, we can make posters, cards, and puppets using crayons. The last thing we see is the fifteen-foot crayon.

"I told you the giant rocking chair was bigger!" says T.J.

"Not by much," I reply. "Lucy, let me take your picture right next to the giant blue crayon."

"I think I should hold a tiny blue crayon from my own box of crayons," Lucy suggests.

Momma thinks it's a great idea. I do, too. When they take my picture, I hold a tiny pink crayon from my box. In the gift shop, we buy postcards. Lucy picks one with a big purple crayon on the front. Then it's time to for me choose a postcard.

That night we camp out one last time. Daddy builds a campfire and we make s'mores. T.J. tells a scary ghost story, but all I can think about is seeing the Queen of Liberty. Just one more day!

Lucy goes into the tent to write a postcard to her Momma.

Dear Momma,

I am having a lot of fun with my best cousin Kylie Jean! Today we went to the Crayon Museum. You know how I like to color. Tomorrow we will be in New York City. Even though road trips are exciting, I am getting a little homesick for all of you. Tomorrow Kylie Jean's dream will come true. We are going to see the Statue of Liberty!

Love you bunches!

Lucy

Chapter Ten
Queen of Liberty

The next day we get a quick start. Everyone is excited! I am going to see the Queen of Liberty! I get out the map. Since we are just over the state line in Pennsylvania, it won't take us long to get to New York State.

Before we know it, Daddy is yelling, "Yee-haw! Next stop, New York City!"

"Yee-haw!" we all yell. We finally made it to New York!

We girls are too excited to play games, color, or chitchat. Even T.J. seems to be excited. He's not even listening to his music. I can hardly believe we are almost to our vacation destination!

Pretty soon the traffic gets thicker and thicker. The cars drive fast, weaving in and out of tiny spots like they are lacing a shoe. I can tell that Daddy is being extra careful at the wheel.

"I sure am glad I'm *not* driving right now," Momma says.

Daddy is doing a mighty fine job. Before we know it, buildings tower over us. We have arrived in New York City.

"Those buildings are taller than the tallest tree in the piney woods!" I say.

T.J. points to the Empire State Building. "That used to be the tallest building in this city, but not anymore," he says.

I can't believe I'm really here. I pinch myself. "Ouch!" I yell.

"Why did you do that?" asks Lucy.

"I can't believe I'm really in the Big Apple!"
I reply.

Soon Daddy finds our hotel. It's called City
Suites. Momma says it is pretty fancy because a
man called a valet parks our car. Once we're in
the hotel, a bellman takes all of our luggage and
delivers it to our room.

Our room has a bedroom with two beds.
Momma and Daddy will sleep in one, and T.J.
will sleep in the other. There is another room with
a tiny kitchen area. It has an itty-bitty refrigerator
and a microwave. On the opposite side of the
room are a couch, TV, and two chairs. The couch
opens up into a bed for Lucy and me.

After we unpack, we change into our special outfits. It is time for us to take the subway to Battery Park.

Momma says, "You picked the perfect tops to wear for a visit to the Statue of Liberty."

"I prefer to think I'm visiting the Queen," I announce. "Queen of Liberty, here I come!"

At the end of the hall
we jump on the elevator,
and I push button one
for the first floor.

We weave through
the crowded lobby and
step out of the hotel
doors. On the street, tall
buildings tower above
us. They are glass and metal giants. Everywhere
around us we hear city noises — honking,
shouting, drilling — and together they make
a kind of music.

Daddy points to the subway sign at the end of
the street. We walk to the entrance and go down a
set of stairs into a tunnel. We wait for the train to
arrive, and then we all step on and take a seat.

It is crowded on the subway. I have never seen so many people all at once. Momma holds Lucy's hand tightly, and Daddy holds mine. T.J. sits close to us, too. The subway train zooms along under the city until we arrive at our stop.

From the subway station, we head to the ferry that will take us to Liberty Island.

The ferryboat is a thousand times bigger than Pa's pontoon boat! While we wait to board, we stand in a building called a terminal.

"Look!" I shout. "Some people are driving their cars onto the boat!"

T.J. is unimpressed. "Let's talk about the good stuff," he says. "This boat has a snack bar!"

"You always think with your stomach," says Momma.

Suddenly, I see her! My whole body is bouncing up and down with excitement. "Oh, Momma, look!" I shout. "There she is!"

"She is gigantic!" says Lucy.

"Wait until you are closer, and she'll look even bigger. She is one hundred and fifty two feet tall," Daddy says.

I am mesmerized by her giant crown and can hardly remember all of my plans. It's a good thing I made a list! I look down at my notes.

1. Check in.

2. Take the tour.

3. Visit the gift shop and get a crown just like the statue!

When we get to Liberty Island, they give us a special red armband and a nickname, too. If you are going on the crown tour, they call you a "Crownie."

"Momma, can you call me a Crownie from now on?" I ask.

She says, "I promise to call you a Crownie all day today!"

We place our bags in a locker in the gift shop. Then we get to skip the long line and go straight through security to the Statue of Liberty's base.

"Sweet!" says T.J. "It's like we're VIP guests."

Finally, our ranger comes over to us. "Hi, I'm Ranger Bob," he says. "You are lucky enough to have crown tickets today! Not everyone gets to tour the crown. There is no elevator in the Statue of Liberty, so we will be climbing three hundred and seventy seven steps to get to the top. Everybody ready?"

"We are!" Lucy and I shout.

Up and up and up we go, climbing steps. It seems like we will never get to the top!

"I'm glad I've been going to the gym!" Momma says.

At the top, the ranger takes our little group into the crown. Lucy and I peer out of small windows.

"You will have only ten minutes, and then we'll make room for the next group," says Ranger Bob.

"Look at the people below us," I say. "They look like ants!"

Then I notice the city rising up across the way. It makes me gasp!

"This view is definitely worth the climb!" Daddy says.

"Amazing!" adds T.J.

"I don't think I can even find the right words to describe how magnificent that skyline is," Momma says.

I don't say anything. No one says anything. We are all quiet — hypnotized by the moment. I've been waiting a long time to visit the Queen of Liberty!

Ranger Bob tells us so many facts about the statue. We'll never remember them all. Did you know they built the arm holding the torch first? I think they should have made the crown first!

"Just a few more minutes," Ranger Bob says, checking his watch.

"Momma, will you please take our picture?" I ask.

"Sure!" says Momma.

Lucy and I pose in front of the window. After the camera flashes, we ask to see the image. There we are — two smiling girls in a tiny square with skyscrapers in the distance. We give Momma a big squeezy hug.

"I'm never going to forget this day!" I say.

Ranger Bob says, "Time to go!"

We climb back down three hundred and seventy seven steps. We are glad climbing down is easier than climbing up!

Last on my list is the gift shop. Momma, T.J., and Lucy are looking at everything, but I only have eyes for the big green foam crown, just like the Queen of Liberty's.

I pull Momma real close. "Momma, can I please get this crown?" I ask.

"I think you must have that crown!" Momma replies. "What else would a Crownie wear?"

I'm so happy, I can hardly stand it. We make our purchases, and Momma places the huge crown on my head. Now I feel like a real, true queen!

Tomorrow Daddy will have his big day, and he will get his award. Then we will go back home to Texas.

We have seen so many things. Some people think that dreams don't come true, but I know better. Standing on the deck of the ferryboat, wearing my colossal crown, I wave good-bye to the Queen of Liberty with my beauty queen wave. I know for sure this has been the best vacation ever!

Marci Bales Peschke was born in Indiana, grew up in Florida, and now lives in Texas with her husband, two children, and a feisty black-and-white cat named Phoebe. She loves reading and watching movies.

When **Tuesday Mourning** was a little girl, she knew she wanted to be an artist when she grew up. Now, she is an illustrator who lives in Utah. She especially loves illustrating books for kids and teenagers. When she isn't illustrating, Tuesday loves spending time with her husband, who is an actor, and their two sons and one daughter.

Glossary

adventure (uhd-VEN-chur)—an exciting experience

atlas (AT-luhs)—a book of maps

attraction (uh-TRAK-shun)—a person or thing that attracts people's attention, admiration, or interest

colossal (kuh-LAH-suhl)—extremely large

destination (des-tuh-NAY-shuhn)—the place to which one is traveling

ferry (FAYR-ee)—a boat or ship that regularly carries people across a stretch of water

liberty (LIB-ur-tee)—another word for freedom

souvenir (SOO-vuh-neer)—an object kept as a reminder of a person, place, or event

valet (va-LAY)—a person who attends to the personal needs of another person

Talk!

1. Kylie Jean uses a road atlas to plan her family's vacation. Ask an adult to help you find an atlas at a library or online. Then map out a route for a vacation you would like to take. Name three other famous tourist attractions in the United States.

2. Why does Kylie Jean call the Statue of Liberty the Queen of Liberty? Do you have a nickname for a special place?

3. What do you think happens on Kylie Jean's trip back to Texas? Tell a friend about it.

Be Creative!

1. Which tourist attraction from the book would you like to visit? Draw a picture of what you think that place looks like.

2. Write three paragraphs about your favorite vacation. Why was it your favorite?

3. Draw a scene from the book that isn't illustrated. Show it to a friend.

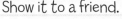

This is the perfect treat for any Vacation Queen!
Just make sure to ask a grown-up for help.

Love, Kylie Jean

From Momma's Kitchen

Big Apple Caramel Pie

YOU NEED:

- 2 premade pie crusts
- 1 cup caramel topping
- 4 tablespoons flour
- 8 cups baking apples
- 1/2 cup brown sugar
- 1 teaspoon ground cinnamon
- a grown-up helper

1. Preheat oven to 400°F.

2. In small bowl, mix caramel topping and 2 tablespoons flour.

3. Put one pie crust in a 9-inch glass pie plate. Spread caramel flour mixture around bottom of pie crust.

4. Ask an adult to peel, core, and slice apples into 1/2- inch pieces. Place apples in large bowl. Add brown sugar, 2 tablespoons flour, and cinnamon to bowl and mix.

5. Spoon mixture into the pie plate and place second pie crust on top.

6. Press along edges of pie crusts to seal together. Ask an adult to make three cuts in the top of the pie crust to allow steam to escape.

7. Bake pie for 60-70 minutes, or until crust is golden brown. Serve after 2 hours of cooling.

Yum, yum!

THE FUN DOESN'T STOP HERE!

Discover more at www.capstonekids.com

- 💜 Videos & Contests
- ✿ Games & Puzzles
- 💜 Friends & Favorites
- ✿ Authors & Illustrators

Find cool websites and more books like this one at www.facthound.com. Just type in the Book ID: **9781515800583** and you're ready to go!